MERCER MAYER'S LITTLE CRITTER®
AT THE BEACH WITH DAD

For Zeb,
Benjamin, Arden and Jessie
who made this
story possible

BY GINA AND MERCER MAYER

inchworm
PRESS

A MERCER MAYER LTD. / J.R. SANSEVERE BOOK

Dad said, "Today we're going to the beach.
Let's get ready."

I ran upstairs and got my Captain Bunny
Snorkle Kit, my Snurfle the Sea Monster
inner tube, my sail boat, my speed boat,
and five power critters.
My little sister only took her Little Miss
Prissy inner tube.

I ran out to the car to put
everything inside.
Then I heard Dad yell out
the window,
"Only take one thing!"

I had to take everything back to my room
except my Captain Bunny Snorkle Kit.
You can't have any real fun anymore.

But Dad took our pail and shovel and
put it in the trunk.
That made me feel better.

Mom packed a picnic lunch and sent us on our way.

"You'll be sorry you didn't come," I called from the car.

"No, I won't," Mom called back. I wondered what she meant.

When we got to the beach, it seemed that everybody else had the same idea. We had to park way far away and carry everything out to the sand.

The sand was hot and it burned our toes.
Dad had to carry my little sister and me.
But he didn't mind because he is strong.

Dad found us a real good spot right
by the waves.
But I thought it was too close.

We all got wet, but I didn't mind because you're supposed to get wet when you're at the beach.

We found a pretty nice spot out by the sidewalk and not really on the sand. It was right next to the Gloopy Snowcone Stand. We all got a snowcone. It was great…

…but I dropped mine into the picnic basket. It made the sandwiches taste better, but no one else thought so.

Dad sat on a nice beach chair. My little sister and I sat on towels. After watching him, I think towels are better.

Little Sister wanted to catch a seagull for a pet,
so she threw some crumbs of bread to one.
Dad didn't think that was a good idea.
We all found out why.

Then we ran down to the water to take
a swim.
I thought it was kinda weird that no
one was in the water.

But Dad said, "Great!" and jumped in.

I guess he didn't see the sign that said
NO SWIMMING TODAY… JELLYFISH.
He only got stung a little.
Dads are so brave — they never cry.

We built the best sand castle I ever saw.
But it was in the way of the sand patrol
jeep. Dad took a picture anyway.

Then Dad said, "I have a great idea.
Follow me."

You know, going to the beach can be a lot of fun, but sometimes a wading pool in the backyard is even better. Dad is so smart!